The Man in the White Robe

ISBN 978-1-0980-9358-7 (paperback)
ISBN 978-1-0980-9359-4 (digital)

Christian Faith Publishing, Inc.
832 Park Avenue
Meadville, PA 16335
www.christianfaithpublishing.com

Printed in the United States of America

The Man in the White Robe

Sandra Darrett

Hi, my name is J-son, and I am eight years old and I am very strong.

I believe that one day, I will be the strongest man in the world. My mommy and daddy always tell me, "J-son be strong," and I try to be every day.

Some days I feel super strong and some days not so much, but I know the world is depending on me to be strong. Sometimes I want to run and play like the other children, but I can't. There are times when I just feel very tired and my body aches every minute and every hour. When that happens, my family tells me to be strong, and they take me to the hospital.

I see my mommy crying a lot, so I try to be strong and brave even when they stick so many different-sized needles in me. Sometimes the nurses give me medicine in the IV attached to my arm, and it makes the pain go away and I can sleep. But today was different; the pain was not going away. The medicine they were giving me now made my body hurt all over and my stomach feel bad.

I didn't like this, and the pain I felt was making me cry. *Mommy, please make them stop. They are hurting me. I want to be strong right now but I can't.* I was trying to wipe away my tears, so I closed my eyes so that my mommy wouldn't see me crying.

I heard my mother talking to the doctors outside my room. She was asking them if there was anything they could do to take away my pain, so they sent in another nurse who gave me something that made me sleep.

Today I dreamt that I was flying through the sky. My cape was flowing in the wind, and the people below me were screaming, “J-son, J-son, J-son, J-son, J-son.” Hearing the people calling my name made me very happy.

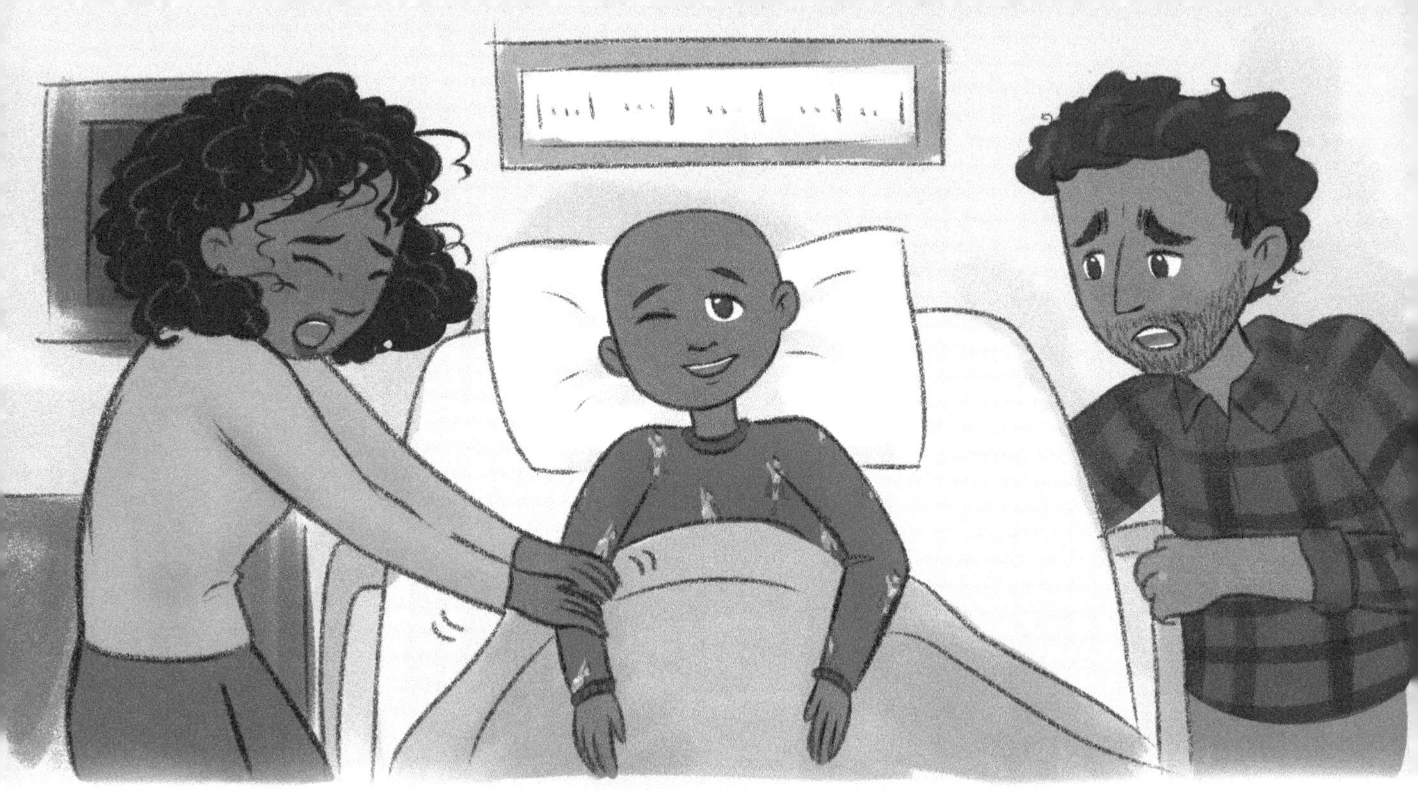

Then I awoke to find that it was my mother calling my name, along with several other doctors in the room. She was sad and crying and saying through her tears, "Don't leave me."

I said, "Mom, don't worry. You have to be brave like me," and I went back to sleep and began flying again.

I was flying over snow-covered mountains. The air was cool as I stretched both my hands out in front of me. I was doing loop-de-loops and flying through the clouds. It felt so nice to feel the mist of the clouds over my face. The sun was shining so bright, and I felt so excited to be going in its direction. The sun was not a fiery ball of heat but a bright, warm yellow ball bouncing in the sky.

As I was flying toward the sun, I looked below and saw the ocean. There were all kinds of ships with people waving at me as I flew by calling my name, “J-son, J-son, J-son, J-son, J-son.” Hearing them call my name made me laugh and giggle, so I smiled and waved back at them.

I decided to fly faster and higher. I was flying so fast even the ocean started splitting beneath me.

I have never seen that before except on the cartoons that I used to watch on TV. I have never felt this free or happy. I was outside in the sun. I wasn't in pain and I even started laughing and doing bigger circles in the sky.

Then I saw it in front of me—a big, beautiful green island. I heard sounds of laughter and cheering. There ahead of me was an island of children calling out to me. They were waving and jumping and shouting my name, "J-son, J-son, J-son, J-son, J-son."

I felt a bright, warm light guiding me to the island. It was calling me and telling me that everything would be all right and to come land and see the beautiful island. So I circled around the island and came in for a landing. As I came closer to the island, I saw so many children waving at me, smiling and laughing and running toward me. I couldn't help but laugh. I have never seen so many smiling children before and children who were happy to see me.

Many children of different shapes and sizes surrounded me, jumping and shouting and holding my hands. I was so giddy—then I saw Him standing there. He was wearing a very bright robe. He shined like the sun itself.

He said, "Come to me, J-son."

I said, "Lord, I will come."

His arms were opened wide and ready to pick me up. I ran as fast as I could and jumped into His arms. He grabbed me and held me tight and told me, “I am very happy to see you.” He kissed my cheek and held me tight again and put me gently down on the grass.

Then He said, “I have been waiting very patiently for you, J-son, to come and be with me. Come and see all that I have for you here.” He carried me into the center of the island full of trees, beautiful flowers, children, and people. He smiled at me and said, “Are you ready to meet everybody?”

I hugged His neck and said yes. He hugged me again, and with a smile on His face, He began to introduce me to everyone.

And in between meeting the different children, He told me with a twinkle in His eyes, “Go! Run and play, for I have taken away all your pain,” and it was true. As I started running, I felt no pain. I couldn’t stop laughing, leaping, jumping, and running. I didn’t want to stop playing with the children. We laughed, danced, hugged, leaped, and chased butterflies. I did all the things I couldn’t do before.

Then as I was about to do leapfrog with the children, a sharp pain made me fall, and I grabbed my stomach. I looked to the Man in the white robe and asked, "What is happening to me?"

He said, "J-son," as He held me close to his chest, "there are people asking for you to return to them."

I said, "I don't want to go back there. There are no children for me to play with. I cannot leap and run and jump. Please don't make me go back."

The Man in the white robe held me tighter and wiped the tears from my eyes and said, "Soon, J-son, soon you will be with us always. I need you to be brave and go back, and I will go with you so that you will not feel the pain."

I slowly opened my eyes to see my mother and father with people I did not know surrounding me. I looked over to them to see the Man in the white robe smiling at me.

My mother pulled me from the hospital bed and cried, “I thought I lost you.” My father and mother kissed my head and laid me back down. Wiping tears from their eyes, they went outside the room to talk to the doctors.

The Man in the white robe said to me, “J-son, your parents love you very much, and they do not want to see you go.

I said, “I know.”

He said, “It’s your choice. If you want to stay, I will go away and come back another day. But if you want to go with me now, I will stand with you as you tell your parents to be brave and you will see them again on another bright and sunny day.”

That made me very happy. The Man in the white robe went to my parents and took them by the hand and brought them to me. As strong as I could, I said, “I love you, Mom, I love you, Dad, but I want to go with the man in the white robe standing by you and me. I need you to be brave like me, and He promised that I will see you again on another bright sunny morning. Please don’t cry. I’m going to be with a lot of children like me. It’s going to be okay.”

My mom and dad hugged me and told me they loved me. The Man in the white robe took my hand, and we were instantly at the island where all the children came and jumped with joy to see me.

My name is J-son, and the Man in the white robe said his name was Jesus and that He came to set me free.

About the Author

Sandra L. Darrett is a mother of five. She has eight grandchildren ranging from one to twenty-seven years old. She has two adopted grandchildren as well. She currently lives in Brooklyn, New York.

She is a member of the Abundant Life Church of God in Christ located in Brooklyn, and she currently does Sunday School lessons on Facebook Live.

CPSIA information can be obtained
at www.ICGtesting.com
Printed in the USA
BVHW021343161121
621766BV00015B/421